My Emotions

SCARED

A Crabtree Roots Book

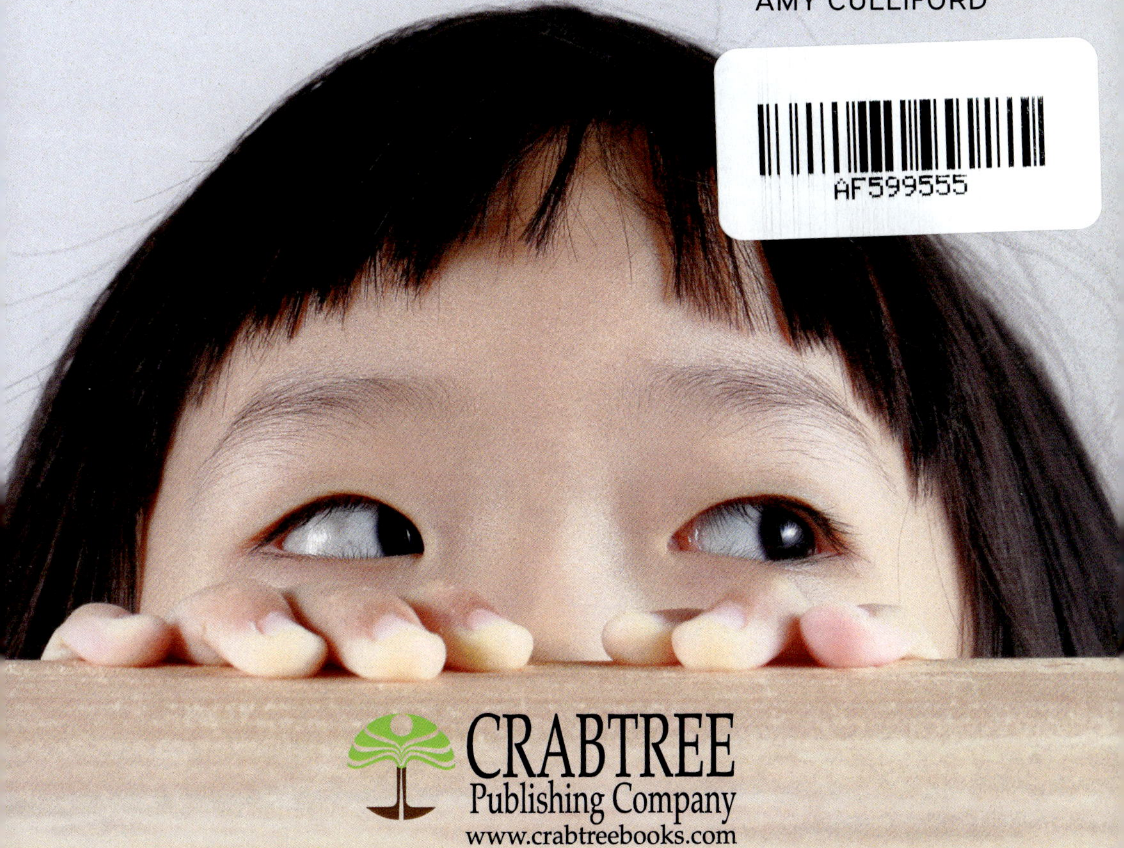

AMY CULLIFORD

School-to-Home Support for Caregivers and Teachers

This book helps children grow by letting them practice reading. Here are a few guiding questions to help the reader with building his or her comprehension skills. Possible answers appear here in red.

Before Reading:

- What do I think this book is about?
    - *This book is about feeling scared.*
    - *This book is about what feeling scared looks or feels like.*

- What do I want to learn about this topic?
    - *I want to learn what to do if I feel scared.*
    - *I want to learn what feeling scared looks like.*

During Reading:

- I wonder why...
    - *I wonder why we cry when we are scared.*
    - *I wonder why trying new things is scary.*

- What have I learned so far?
    - *I have learned that scared is an emotion.*
    - *I have learned that some people yell when they are scared.*

After Reading:

- What details did I learn about this topic?
    - *I have learned that it is good to tell someone you are scared.*
    - *I have learned that everyone can feel scared about something.*

- Read the book again and look for the vocabulary words.
    - *I see the word **hide** on page 6 and the word **storms** on page 8. The other vocabulary words are found on page 14.*

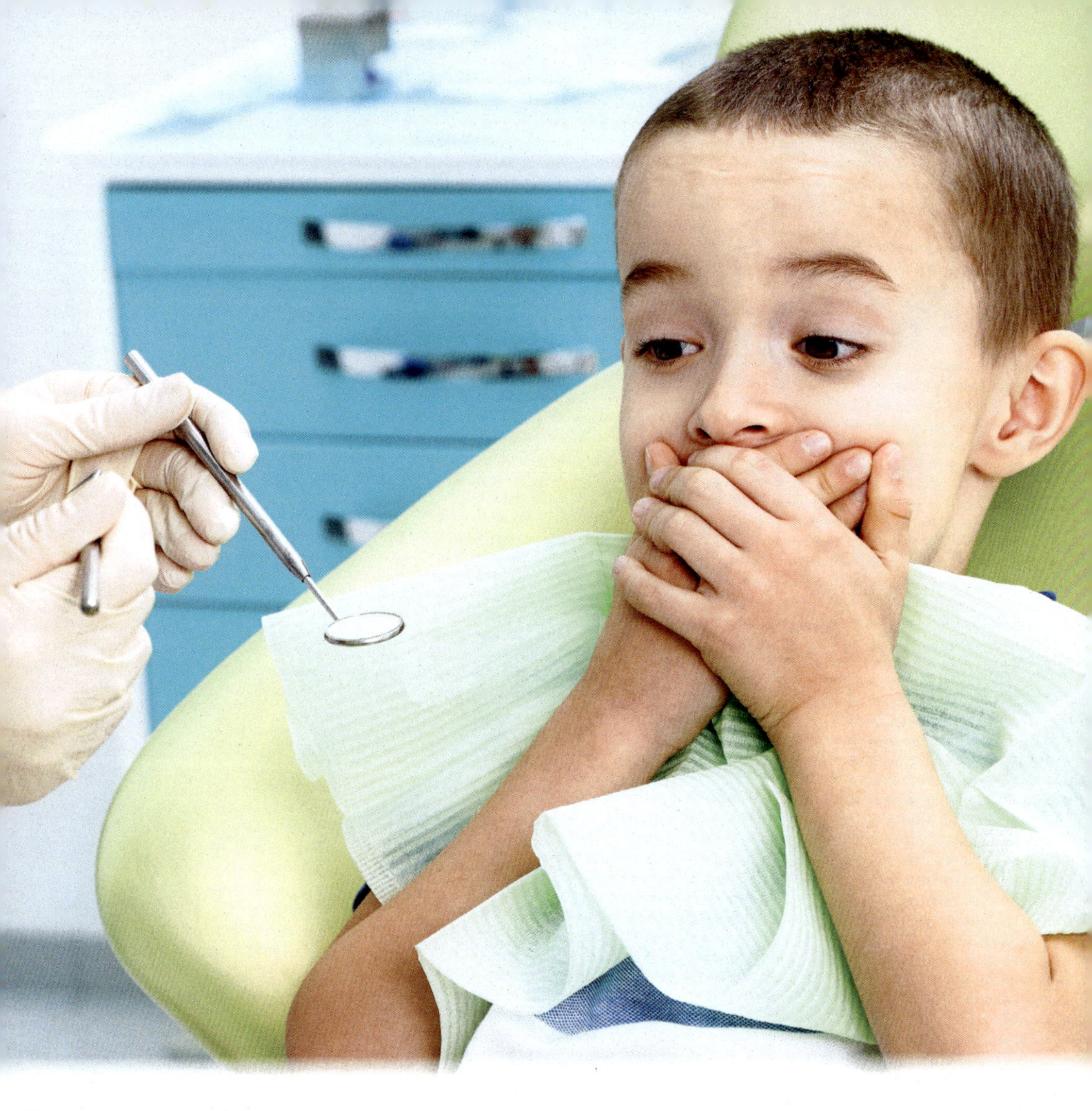

What **scares** you?

I am scared of
the **dark**.

I **hide** when I
am scared.

I am scared of **storms.**

I **cry** when am I
am scared.

I go find my **mom**
when I am scared.

What scares you?

Word List

Sight Words

am	I	what
find	of	when
go	the	you

Words to Know

cry

dark

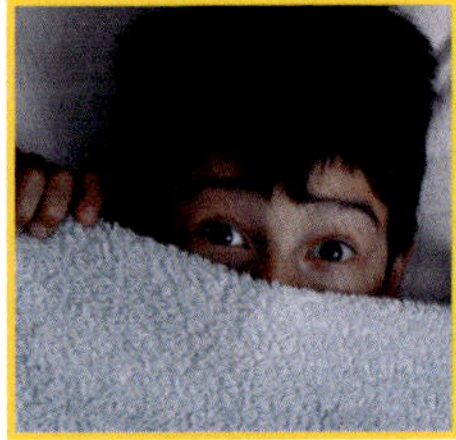

hide

mom

scares

storms

38 Words

What **scares** you?

I am scared of the **dark**.

I **hide** when I am scared.

I am scared of **storms**.

I **cry** when I am scared.

I go find my **mom** when I am scared.

What scares you?

CRABTREE Publishing Company

Written by: Amy Culliford
Designed by: Rhea Wallace
Series Development: James Earley
Proofreader: Ellen Rodger
Educational Consultant: Marie Lemke M.Ed.

Photographs:
Shutterstock: Juan Pablo Gonzaález: cover; TY Ilm: p. 1; Aleksandr Rybalko: p. 3, 14; Kryzhov: p. 5, 14; justoomm: p. 7, 14; HelloRF Zcool: p. 8, 14; fizkes: p. 9, 14; Inna Ska: p. 13

Library and Archives Canada Cataloguing in Publication
Title: Scared / Amy Culliford.
Names: Culliford, Amy, 1992- author.
Description: Series statement: My emotions | "A Crabtree roots book".
Identifiers: Canadiana (print) 20210156570 | Canadiana (ebook) 20210156589 | ISBN 9781427139672 (hardcover) | ISBN 9781427139733 (softcover) | ISBN 9781427133410 (HTML) | ISBN 9781427139795 (read-along ebook) | ISBN 9781427134011 (EPUB)
Subjects: LCSH: Fear in children—Juvenile literature. | LCSH: Fear—Juvenile literature.
Classification: LCC BF723.F4 C85 2021 | DDC j152.4/6—dc23

Library of Congress Cataloging-in-Publication Data
Names: Culliford, Amy, 1992- author.
Title: Scared / Amy Culliford.
Description: New York : Crabtree Publishing, 2021. | Series: My emotions, a crabtree roots book | Includes index.
Identifiers: LCCN 2021009533 (print) | LCCN 2021009534 (ebook) | ISBN 9781427139672 (hardcover) | ISBN 9781427139733 (paperback) | ISBN 9781427139795 (read along) | ISBN 9781427133410 (ebook) | ISBN 9781427134011 (epub)
Subjects: LCSH: Fear--Juvenile fiction. | Emotions--Juvenile fiction.
Classification: LCC BF575.F2 .C85 2021 (print) | LCC BF575.F2 (ebook) | DDC 155.4/1246--dc23
LC record available at https://lccn.loc.gov/2021009533
LC ebook record available at https://lccn.loc.gov/2021009534

Crabtree Publishing Company
www.crabtreebooks.com 1-800-387-7650

Printed in Canada/092022/CPC20220913

 In Canada: We acknowledge the financial support of the Government of Canada through the Canada Book Fund for our publishing activities.

Published in the United States
Crabtree Publishing
347 Fifth Avenue, Suite 1402-145
New York, NY, 10016

Published in Canada
Crabtree Publishing
616 Welland Ave.
St. Catharines, Ontario L2M 5V6